for our Salties

Thanks for the continued love and support. You make the journey worth it.

WHEN A LLAMA GETS LOOSE
WRITTEN BY CHASE SALT PICKETT
ILLUSTRATED BY JENN SCOTT PICKETT
PUBLISHED BY SME PUBLISHING

WWW.SALTYMERMAIDENTERTAINMENT.COM

ISBN: 978-1-7360152-0-9

SME PUBLISHING
TEXT COPYRIGHT © 2020 JAMES CHASE PICKETT
ILLUSTRATION COPYRIGHT © 2020 JENNIFER SCOTT PICKETT

WHEN A LLAMA GETS LOOSE

WRITTEN BY CHASE SALT PICKETT
ILLUSTRATED BY JENN SCOTT PICKETT

So calm and so quiet, as it sits in its pen.

It might beg to come out, but you must not give in!

Don't be fooled by the smile.

It's all just a ruse...

'Cause a llama goes

CRAZY

when a llama gets loose!

When a llama
gets loose,
your food is
not safe.
It will gobble
your snacks!
It will break all your
plates!

It'll **hiccup**

and **burp**

after drinking
Mom's juice,

'cause a llama goes
crazy

when a llama gets
loose.

When a llama gets loose, it will break all your toys...

But YOU'LL
be in trouble
for making the
noise.

It will paint on the walls and eat your dad's shoes...

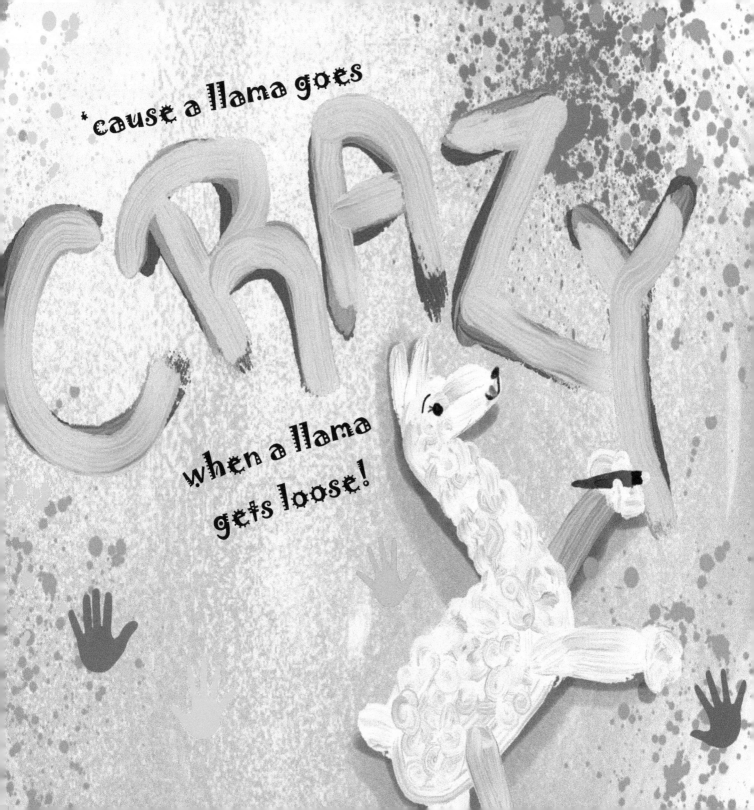

When a llama gets loose, you'll find its ~~butt~~ in your bath. It will gargle your bubbles! It will surf! It will *splash*!

It will make giant waves
'til you beg for a truce.

'Cause a llama goes crazy
when a llama gets loose.

When a llama gets loose,

it refuses to sleep.

It steals all your covers.

It farts in your sheets.

You'll get pushed off the bed by its fuzzy caboose.
'Cause a llama goes crazy when a llama gets loose.

When a llama gets loose,
your life is a mess.

It's caused ~~trouble~~ all day,
now you can't even rest.

You must think of a plan, because there's one thing we know.

All this llama drama has to

go go GO

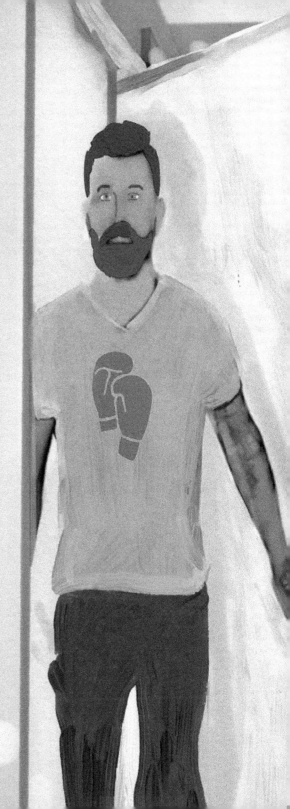

Hmmm...

With cookies and cakes and a trail of snacks,
you'll lead it back in...

Then **WHAM!**

It'll be trapped!

Phew!

We love our *silly llama*, and we did have some fun.

But we're glad that it's resting and the day is all done.

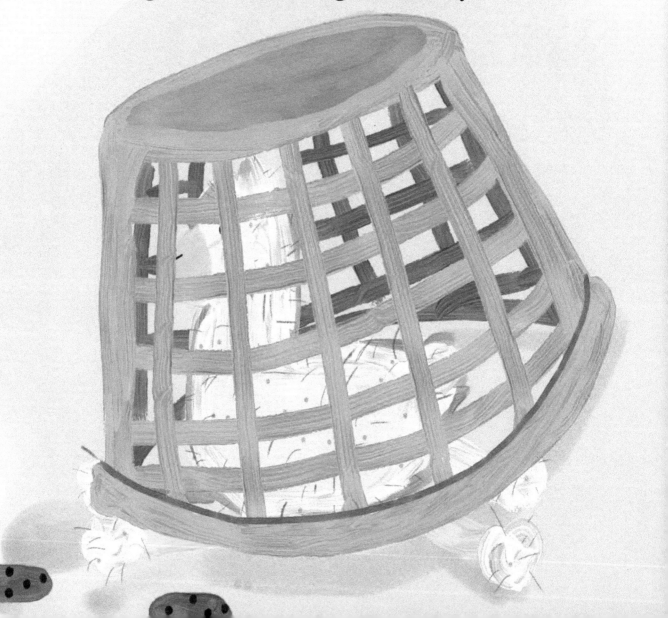

Don't be fooled by its closed eyes

or its cute little snooze...

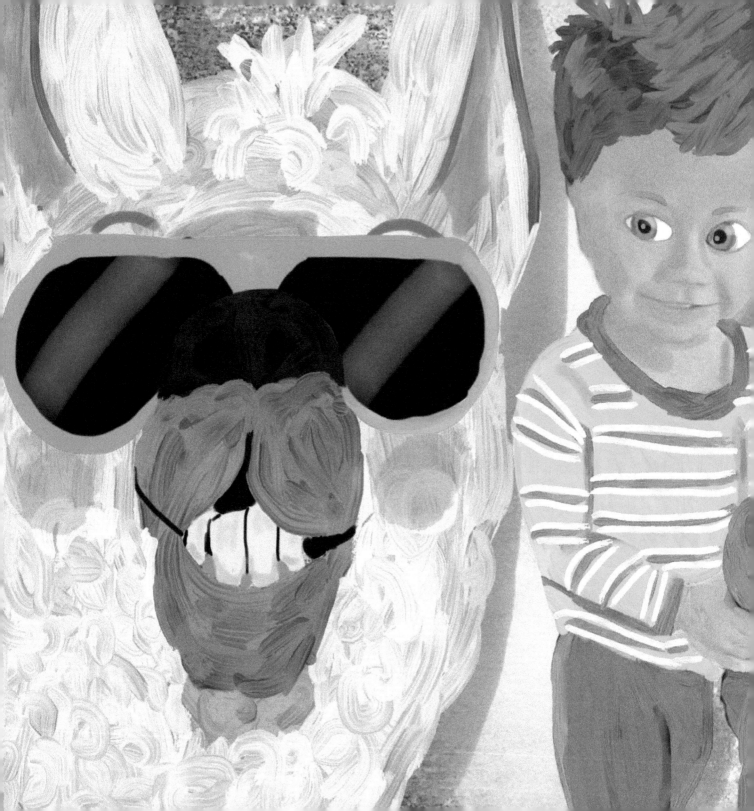

'Cause a llama
ALWAYS goes

CRAZY

when a llama
gets loose!

A WORD FROM THE CREATORS

Thanks for reading our book! If you enjoyed it (you did enjoy it... right?) please leave a positive review. Your support makes a huge difference.

We'd love to connect with you online. We create a lot of free funny content, so be sure to check out our website and find us on social media. Stay salty!

Love,

Jenn & Chase

CPSIA information can be obtained
at www.ICGtesting.com
Printed in the USA
LVHW072242020221
678126LV00006B/129